Wishes really do come true

Lucky Stars

The Pop Singer Wish

Phoebe Bright

Illustrated by Karen Donnelly

MACMILLAN CHILDREN'S BOOKS

With special thanks to Maria Faulkner

First published 2012 by Macmillan Children's Books
a division of Macmillan Publishers Limited
20 New Wharf Road, London N1 9RR
Basingstoke and Oxford
Associated companies throughout the world
www.panmacmillan.com

ISBN 978-1-4472-0235-6

1 3 5 7 9 8 6 4 2

A CIP catalogue record for this book is available from the British Library.

Printed and bound by CPI Group (UK) Ltd, Croydon CR0 4YY

With thanks to all the magical people in my life for their belief in me

Racecourse
Daffodil Farm
Pigsty
B&B
Town Hal
Starwatcher Towers B&B
Orchard
Beach

Whimsy Woods
Strawberry Field
Library
Flashley Manor Hotel
ry-cake Bakery
Fancy-dress Shop
Bert's Donkey Stables
Pier

Contents

Hello, friend!

I'm Stella Starkeeper and I want to tell you a secret. Have you ever gazed up at the stars and thought how magical they looked? Well, you're right. Stars really do have magic!

Their precious glittering light allows me to fly down from the sky, all the way to Earth. You see, I'm always on the lookout for boys and girls who are especially kind and helpful. I train them to become Lucky Stars - people who can make wishes come true!

So the next time you're under the twinkling night sky, look out for me. I'll be floating among the stars somewhere. Do give me a wave!

Love from
Stella x

1

Songs on the Sand

'*Magic, magic moments, these are magic moments* . . .' Cassie sang.

Her black and white cat, Twinkle, joined in. 'Yowl, yowl, meow, yowl . . .'

The huge dome of the observatory at Starwatcher Towers rang with the sounds of their voices. Cassie was singing along to a CD of 'Magic Moments', the latest hit by Jacey Day. She was Cassie's favourite pop star, and that afternoon Cassie and her friend Kate were going to watch Jacey perform. She was the opening act in the Songs on the Sand music festival, right here in Astral-on-Sea!

All week, Cassie and Kate had been practising a special dance routine to 'Magic Moments'. As she twirled, Cassie imagined that Kate was also dancing around the Fairy-cake Bakery where she lived with her mum.

Cassie turned up the music. 'Let's dance, Twinkle,' she giggled.

Twinkle blinked his eyes. Cassie scooped him up from the old leather chair in which he was sitting and whirled across the room, being careful not to bump into any of the shiny telescopes. Her dad was an astronomer, and most nights he could be

found up here, watching the stars.

'There's a friend I'd love to meet,
Spinning world beneath his feet,
He's got pebbles in his hands,
Running across the glistening sands . . .'

Along with Jacey's sweet, clear voice, the backing singers added a catchy harmony to the song. Their voices blended together perfectly.

When the song ended, Cassie noticed a tingling feeling in her arm. She put Twinkle back on the chair and looked at the charm bracelet round her wrist. Her new butterfly charm seemed to flutter its colourful wings.

'I wonder what magical power this charm has,' Cassie said. 'And who I'll help next.'

Cassie used her magical charms to help make people's wishes come true. With each person that she helped, she received another charm for her bracelet. So far Cassie had three. The bird charm gave her the power to fly and the crescent moon allowed her to talk to animals. But the magic of the butterfly was still a mystery.

'Meow!' Twinkle's ears twitched. He seemed to be trying to tell her something.

Cassie concentrated hard on her crescent-moon charm, so she could understand him. 'What is it, Twinkle?' she asked.

'I can hear music,' he said. His ears twitched again. 'It's coming from outside.'

Cassie listened. Yes, there *was* music, a beautiful tinkling sound. Where was it coming from? She gazed up into the brilliant blue sky and saw a star shining brightly at her. Cassie knew how unusual it was to see a star in daylight, but she also knew this was no ordinary star.

The star zoomed down, straight through the open skylight of the dome, filling the observatory with silvery music. Then, with a *whizz* and a *fizz* and a *zip-zip-zip*, it landed next to Cassie.

'Meow!' Twinkle shot under the chair.

Cassie watched with delight as the star grew into a column of dazzling light, which slowly changed into . . .

'Stella Starkeeper!' Cassie flung her arms round her friend. 'It's *so* good to see you!'

Stella was helping Cassie to become a Lucky Star. Today she looked as lovely as ever, her silver dress and leggings glittering

above her shiny boots and her long silver hair rippling over her shoulders.

'I see you've earned your third charm,' Stella said. 'Well done. You'll soon have all seven charms and become a Lucky Star. Then you'll be able to grant wishes whenever you like!'

'I can't wait,' said Cassie. She turned the little butterfly in her fingers and looked at its glittery wings. 'But what does my new charm do?'

Twinkle crept out from under the chair and tried to bat the little charm with his paw.

Stella laughed and tickled Twinkle under the chin, making him purr loudly. 'I'll give you a clue,' she said, her velvety-blue eyes shining. 'You have all the time in the world . . .'

The beautiful music filled the dome again. With a wave, Stella disappeared in a shower of glittering sparkles.

Cassie looked at Twinkle. '*All the time in the world*. I wonder what Stella could mean?'

2
Mystery Guests

Cassie ran down the stairs to the ground floor, jumping the final three steps. At the same moment, Mum came out of the kitchen carrying a tray with a jug of iced water, some freshly baked cakes and a lovely bunch of flowers. Cassie stopped just in time – one more step and they would have crashed!

'Careful, darling,' said Mum. 'You nearly flew into me.'

Cassie gave a secret smile. Good thing she hadn't used her bird charm to *really* fly down the stairs!

'Sorry, Mum,' she said, holding the dining-room door open for her.

'I heard you having a good sing-song,' Cassie's dad said with a grin. 'Are you sure Jacey Day wasn't up there with you?'

Cassie giggled and looked at the dining table Dad was polishing. Her brown eyes and fair hair were reflected in its gleaming surface. 'Wow, it's as shiny as a mirror!' she said.

'We're just getting ready for some surprise guests,' Dad explained. 'The booking only came through this morning.'

Starwatcher Towers was a bed and

breakfast, as well as an observatory.

'The tourist board was very hush-hush, like it's some sort of secret,' said Mum. 'All they told us is that the guests are a mum and daughter who need lots of privacy.'

'We don't even know their names!' Dad added.

'Very mysterious,' Cassie said.

'All mysteries can be solved, as long as you carefully examine the facts,' said a familiar voice behind her.

Cassie turned to see Alex standing in the hallway with his little white puppy, Comet. She grinned at him. Alex and his parents were on holiday at the B & B. He was obsessed with science, and at first hadn't believed in Stella Starkeeper and Cassie's magical bracelet. But he soon changed his mind, and he and Cassie had become firm friends.

Ring-ring! Ring-ring!

'Yupp! Yupp!' Comet leaped around the hallway, barking at the ringing telephone.

'Sit, Comet. Good boy,' Alex said,

stroking his excited puppy.

Comet flopped down, wagging his tail, as Cassie's mum answered the phone.

'Hello. Starwatcher Towers. Can I help you?' Mum said. 'Oh, hello, love.' She paused, her smile turning into a worried frown. 'Oh dear. Yes, of course I'll tell Cassie. I hope Kate's feeling better soon.'

'What's wrong with Kate?' Cassie asked, when her mum had put the phone down.

'She can still go to the concert, can't she?'

Mum shook her head. 'I'm afraid not. Her mum says she's tucked up in bed with a sore throat.'

'Poor Kate. She must be so disappointed to miss seeing Jacey Day.' Cassie gave a heavy sigh. 'Our song-and-dance routine is nearly perfect now.'

'What a shame,' Mum said, giving Cassie a hug. 'You'll have to sing twice as loud. Maybe you could do something nice to cheer Kate up.'

Cassie nodded but still felt disappointed.

Comet ran over and licked Cassie's toes, as if trying to make her feel better. Cassie couldn't help smiling.

'I think Comet wants to go to the concert with you,' Alex laughed.

This gave Cassie an idea . . .

'Would *you* like to go to the concert with me, Alex?' she asked hopefully. 'I've got the tickets already.'

'Really?' Alex's brown eyes seemed to light up. 'Yes, please! I've never been to a

concert before, so it'll be a bit like a science experiment, won't it?'

Cassie clapped her hands in delight and did a little twirl down the hallway. Alex grinned.

Ding-dong! The doorbell jangled through the hall. Mum hurried to answer it. 'Looks like our mystery guests have arrived,' she said.

Cassie felt a flutter of excitement. Who could they be?

'Hello,' Cassie's mum said to the tall, slim woman standing on the doorstep. 'Welcome to Starwatcher Towers.'

Just beyond her, Cassie could see a teenage girl with long dark hair. She was wearing skinny jeans, a cropped pink jacket and glittery silver shoes. Cassie smiled at her and the girl gave a wave back.

'It's so nice to be here,' the woman said. 'My daughter and I have had a long journey.'

'Come in and make yourselves at home,' Mum said, holding the door open.

The woman smiled at Cassie as she walked past in her high-heeled shoes,

leaving a faint whiff of perfume behind her. Dad helped carry in their two smart suitcases.

Outside, the woman's daughter had wandered on to the lawn and was speaking quietly into her mobile phone.

'Wow,' Cassie whispered to Alex. 'She looks like a film star with those big sunglasses.'

'I think she's a famous scientist,' Alex

replied. 'See that phone? It's very hi-tech. Does all sorts of things.'

'I love her shiny hair,' Cassie sighed. 'And her silver shoes. Our mystery guests are so glamorous!'

Alex adjusted his glasses, as if trying to get a better look. 'Really?' he said. 'Their clothes look pretty normal to me.'

Cassie grinned to herself. Alex would only notice someone's outfit if it was a lab coat and science goggles!

Cassie knew it wasn't polite to stare, but she couldn't seem to tear her eyes away from the girl. Even though she couldn't see the girl's face, Cassie felt sure she had seen her somewhere before. But where?

3
Jacey Day!

Cassie and Alex watched from the front step as the girl finished her call and glanced at the gold watch on her wrist. She paced the lawn, her forehead creased with worry.

'I wonder what's wrong?' said Cassie quietly.

'It looks like she's had some bad news,' said Alex. 'Maybe she's the person you're supposed to help.'

Cassie shook her head. 'She's so

glamorous. She doesn't need *me* to make a wish come true!'

At last, the girl walked over towards Cassie and Alex. 'Hi,' she said with a grin.

'Hi,' Cassie replied, suddenly feeling a bit shy. 'I'm Cassie and this is Alex.'

'Um . . . hello,' said Alex.

'It's very nice to meet you,' the girl said. But to Cassie's surprise, she didn't tell them her name. Instead, she pointed to Cassie's wrist. 'I like your charm bracelet. I've never seen one like it before.'

'Thank you.' Cassie jingled her bracelet and smiled. The girl couldn't possibly know how special it really was!

'I . . . er . . . heard about the Songs on the

Sand festival today. Do you know how to get there?' the girl asked.

'Alex and I can show you the way to the beach,' Cassie said. 'We'll be going there soon.'

'Have you got a ticket?' Alex asked the girl.

'Don't worry,' she said. 'I won't need a ticket.'

Cassie and Alex exchanged a surprised look. Why wouldn't the girl need a ticket?

Whoever she is, Cassie thought, *she's very mysterious . . .*

Having arranged to meet their parents at the festival later, Cassie, Alex and the girl headed for the beach. Comet bounded beside them.

Cassie pointed at a cluster of tents in the distance. 'You can see the festival from here,' she said as they walked down the hill.

'There's a fun fair as well!' Alex said before Comet tugged on his lead, pulling Alex ahead of the two girls.

'You seem so familiar,' Cassie told the other girl. 'I'm sure I've seen you before.'

The girl didn't reply, but pushed her sunglasses further up the bridge of her nose.

'Sorry, I don't know your name?' Cassie asked.

'Oh, yes . . . I'm Jacinta,' the girl replied. 'Thanks for showing me to the festival.'

Alex ran back towards them. 'Look at that crowd!' he said. 'I estimate there must be at least a thousand people!'

They all ran down the last part of the hill and on to the promenade. Cassie felt her

heart quicken with excitement – she would be seeing Jacey Day soon! She started to sing 'Magic Moments'.

'When the city's far away,
Then the sunshine fills my day . . .'

Jacinta gave a curious smile. 'That's a Jacey Day song,' she said.

'Yes, she's fantastic,' Cassie said. 'I can't wait to see her in concert today!'

But Cassie noticed that Jacinta's forehead had creased up with worry again.

As they hurried along the promenade, Cassie waved to Bert, who was giving donkey rides to the children on the beach. At last they reached the festival gates, where a huge billboard showed the list of singers and when they were due to perform. Jacey Day's name was first.

'Look,' Cassie said, pointing at the billboard. 'Perfect timing – Jacey's on soon!'

Jacinta just nodded, looking even more worried than before.

What could be the problem? Cassie wondered. *I don't know how to help unless I can find out what's wrong.*

An official-looking man carrying a clipboard walked up to the gates. As he approached, he spoke into a mobile phone. Cassie noticed that Jacinta was tapping her foot anxiously.

'Yep,' the man said. 'I've found her. I'll let her know.'

He beckoned for them to come through the gates. Cassie and Alex showed their tickets, but Jacinta was allowed straight through.

'Have you found anyone else?' she asked the man in a quiet voice.

'No, I'm sorry. It's hard to find replacements at this short notice,' he told her.

Jacinta's face fell. 'But it will be a disaster without them,' she declared. 'Please try again.'

'I wonder what's going to be a disaster,' Cassie whispered to Alex.

The man spoke into his phone, waited for an answer and then shook his head.

'Sorry, there's no chance. I'm afraid you'll have to do it on your own. Or cancel,' he said.

Cancel what? thought Cassie.

Jacinta turned away and covered her face with her hands. Tears were trickling down her cheeks.

'Oh, please don't cry!' Cassie exclaimed. From her pocket, she pulled out a tissue decorated with colourful stars, and offered it to Jacinta.

'Thanks,' Jacinta sobbed.

She took off her sunglasses and wiped the tears from her eyes.

Cassie's heart did a flip-flop of excitement. She couldn't believe it! Jacinta was none other than her favourite pop star, Jacey Day!

4
All the Time in the World

Still clutching Cassie's tissue, Jacey slipped her sunglasses back on before anyone else recognized her.

'I've worked it out!' Alex said, hopping up and down with excitement. 'Jacey must be short for Jacinta. Wow, I've never met a famous person before!'

Cassie could barely contain herself either. She had so many questions she wanted to ask Jacey, like what her favourite colour was and if she had any pets.

'I can't believe you're staying with us!' she cried. 'Starwatcher Towers is only a small bed and breakfast. Why aren't you staying at a posh hotel like Flashley Manor?'

'I liked the name,' Jacey replied. 'And it's so cool that it's an observatory too. Anyway, it gets difficult at the big hotels. Mum thought it would be a good idea to try a place where I'd attract less attention.'

She smiled at Cassie, but then looked sad again as a boy and girl walked past. They were wearing 'I LOVE JACEY' T-shirts.

'Jacey Day's on soon,' the boy was saying. 'We'd better hurry.'

Jacey looked at her watch. 'Oh dear, there isn't time to sort anything out. I'm going to let down everyone who's come to see the start of the festival.'

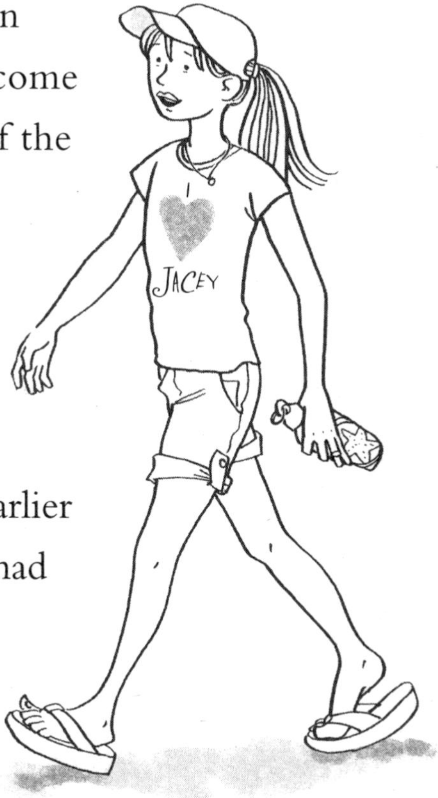

'Why?' Cassie asked. 'What's happened?'

'My backing singers phoned earlier to say they both had sore throats and they weren't sure if they could sing,' Jacey explained. 'The man with the headphones is the festival manager. He told me they're definitely too ill to come and he hasn't been able to find replacements.'

Just like Kate, Cassie thought.

'I'm so upset,' Jacey continued. 'All summer I've been looking forward to being the opening act at Songs on the Sands. And, you know, this is such a lovely place, it almost seems as if "Magic Moments" was meant especially for Astral-on-Sea.'

'Isn't there anything we can do?' asked Cassie. 'Perhaps Alex and I can help.'

'I don't think so, but thanks.' Jacey gave a deep sigh. 'You've heard the song, haven't you? I sing the melody, but it's the backing singers who give the song rhythm with their harmony. "Magic Moments" won't work without the backing singers.'

Cassie thought back to being in the observatory with Twinkle, singing and dancing to the CD. She knew that Jacey was right.

'My fans will be disappointed if I don't sing my hit song,' said Jacey. 'I really wish I could perform "Magic Moments" here.'

Cassie and Alex glanced at one another. Jacey had made her wish – to sing 'Magic Moments' at the Songs on the Sand festival. Cassie couldn't believe it. So Jacey Day really *did* need her help! But how could she make her wish come true?

Cassie looked at her charm bracelet. It was glittering in the sunlight, her new butterfly charm spinning slowly in the breeze. She had to work out what the charm could do.

'I've got an idea,' Cassie said. 'We could stage auditions. There are plenty of people here, so there's bound to be someone who can sing "Magic Moments" with you.'

Jacey glanced at her watch. 'Backing singers would need all the time in the world to learn the harmonies, and I'm supposed to go onstage in a few minutes. It's no good, I'll have to cancel.'

Cassie gasped. What had Jacey just said? *All the time in the world . . .*

She could guess now what Stella Starkeeper's clue had meant – and the magical power of her new charm!

Gazing at the tiny butterfly, Cassie concentrated hard. The charm sparkled brightly, sending rainbows of colour into the air. The tiny wings flapped rhythmically – one, two, one, two, just like the ticking hands of a clock.

All around her people stopped, standing as still as statues. A seagull froze in mid-flight. In the ice-cream queue, a boy who

was pulling funny faces was now stuck with his tongue out! Comet, looking as cute as ever, stood on his hind legs with his front paws in the air, tail frozen in mid-wag. It was like pressing the pause button on her DVD player. Nothing moved. Everywhere was still and silent.

Amazing, thought Cassie. *Now I really can make Jacey's wish come true. I've got all the time in the world!*

5
Song and Dance

Jacey and Alex also stood frozen in front of Cassie. Jacey's forehead was puckered with worry, and Alex had his mouth open, as if he was about to speak.

Oh no, Cassie thought. *How do I unfreeze Alex and no one else?*

She put her hand on his arm. 'I'm going to need your help, Alex,' she said. 'I wish you would wake up!'

Immediately, Alex came to life.

'Whoa!' he cried, staring around at the still, silent crowd of people. 'What happened?'

'It's my butterfly charm,' said Cassie. 'It gives me the power to stop time.'

Alex shook his head in disbelief. 'But that's not scientifically possible.'

'It's not science,' Cassie reminded him. 'It's magic.'

She leant down and touched Comet on the top of his furry head. 'I wish you would wake up too, Comet.'

The little puppy immediately wagged his tail. 'Yupp!' he barked in surprise.

'Come on, follow me!' she said to Alex. 'I've got an idea.'

They left Jacey standing frozen to the spot and ran towards the fairground stalls. 'We need some costumes,' said Cassie.

'Costumes?' echoed Alex. 'What for?'

'You'll see,' answered Cassie, plonking a big straw hat with the Songs on the Sand logo on his head. She put one on her own head, then added a pair of sparkly sunglasses, and looked in the stallholder's mirror.

Alex straightened up the hat, and then tried on a pair of sunglasses with bright blue lenses. 'What do you think?'

'Perfect!' said Cassie.

Taking out her purse, she left some of her pocket money on the stand. Then she ran up a flight of wooden steps that led to the area behind the stage. There were big spotlights on stands, speakers and frozen festival organizers. Cassie

stashed the hats and sunglasses behind a woman wearing headphones, then ran back to where Jacey was still standing frozen in time.

'Right,' Cassie said, turning to Alex. 'Now we've got a lot of practice to do if we're going to be Jacey's backing singers.'

'We're going to sing? In front of all these people?' Alex gulped.

'Yes,' Cassie said excitedly. She looked around at the huge audience that had gathered to see Jacey Day's performance. 'We're going to help Jacey's wish come true!'

Alex was quiet for a moment. Then he said, 'But, Cassie, I don't even know the words to "Magic Moments". Besides,

although I quite like singing to myself in the bath, I get scared in front of lots of people. I'll sound awful!'

Cassie's face fell. Maybe her plan wasn't

going to work after all. She looked at Alex, nervously hopping from foot to foot, then at the frozen tears on Jacey's face.

'But we've got to do it,' she declared. 'Don't worry, Alex. I'll teach you the words to "Magic Moments". Then we'll work on the rest. Please,' she added. 'I can't make Jacey's wish come true without you!'

'Then I'll give it a go,' Alex said. 'You're my friend and I want to help.'

Cassie grinned at Alex and started to sing:

'Kids are building castles high
With candyfloss and ice-cream smiles . . .'

Alex listened. Then he tried to sing the words back to her:

'Kids are building candy high
With something, something and dreamy
smiles . . .'

He kept getting the lines wrong!

'Oh dear,' Cassie said. 'I don't think I'm teaching you very well.'

She sat in one of the deckchairs, next to a lady whose ice-cream drips were hovering in mid-air.

Alex slumped into the chair on her other side. 'I'm sorry, Cassie. I can write out a complicated maths sum and know it off by heart, but I can't seem to remember the words to a song.'

'That's it!' Cassie said. 'If I write down the words to the song, you'll remember

them better. Have you got your notebook and pen with you?'

Alex pulled them out of his pocket and handed them over.

Cassie wrote the words out and she and Alex practised them over and over again.

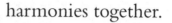

'That's much better,' Cassie said, once Alex had sung the words correctly all the way through. 'Now we need to practise the harmonies together. But if I'm singing as well, then I won't be able to tell if it sounds right.'

Just then, Comet sat in front of them. He placed his chin on Alex's knee.

Alex grinned. 'Let's ask Comet to help.'

'Comet?' Cassie giggled, remembering Twinkle's singing earlier in the day. 'But he's a puppy. He can't sing!'

They both looked at Comet. Ears pricked, he wagged his tail, making his whole body wiggle. Cassie could tell that he thought something interesting was going on.

'Yes, it's true,' Alex said. 'He can't sing. But dogs do have special hearing – sort of super-sensitive. They can move their ears in different directions to pick up more sounds than us.'

'So, Comet can tell us whether he thinks we sound good or not,' said Cassie. 'Great idea, Alex!'

6
Practice Makes Perfect

Cassie thought hard about her crescent-moon charm, which let her talk to animals. Sparkles swirled around the bracelet and danced around Comet's head.

'Comet, we need your help,' said Cassie.

'Hooray!' Comet yipped. 'What do you want me to do?'

'We need you to listen to Alex and me singing "Magic Moments". Can you tell us how we sound together and if we're singing in tune?' Cassie asked.

'Yep, I can do that. No problem!' Comet replied. He rushed around the deckchairs, then leaped on to one of them and sat with his ears pricked. 'I'm ready,' he said.

Cassie laughed. 'Thanks, Comet.' She turned to Alex. 'Let's try singing it together – onstage this time.'

They climbed on to the stage. Cassie weaved through the people setting up the music equipment, who were

all frozen in time. Carefully, she took a microphone out of the stand it was resting in. Alex borrowed his microphone from a woman whose tinted glasses were almost falling off her nose.

On the count of three, Cassie started to sing. '*Magic, magic moments . . .*'

'Good, Cassie,' Comet barked from the front row. 'But I can hardly hear Alex. He's mumbling.'

'Alex, Comet says you need to sing louder,' Cassie told him. 'You've got to sing loudly enough for the people in the back row to hear you.'

'But it's scary singing to all these people,' he said.

Cassie thought for a moment. 'You said

you like singing to yourself in the bath, right?'

Alex nodded.

'Well, pretend you're singing to yourself

but in a great big bathtub,' said Cassie, 'the biggest in the world!'

Alex laughed. They started the song again, and this time, Cassie could hear his singing get louder and louder as he became more confident. Soon he was belting out his lines, matching Cassie's soaring voice.

'Magic, magic moments.
These are magic moments . . .'

'I never knew I could sing like that,' Alex said with a big grin when they had sung the last notes. 'It's fun!'

'Well, I think you're really good,' said Cassie. 'Let's see what Comet thinks.'

'Hooray!' barked the little puppy.

'You both sounded fantastic!'

Cassie smiled. They were almost ready to start time again.

'Now we'll just add the dance steps,' she told Alex.

'I'm really not very good at dancing,' Alex said, gulping again. 'But I suppose I'll give it a go. After all, until today I didn't think I was very good at singing either.'

Cassie grinned at Alex. He was trying so hard to be a good friend and to help Jacey. She danced around the band members, waving at the frozen drummer who looked as if he was smiling at them. Alex followed, copying Cassie's routine. Then she noticed him adding his own moves.

'What do you think of this, Cassie?' he

said. 'I'm calling it the sound wave.' He did a rippling arm movement. 'And this move is like a clock ticking.' He hopped from foot to foot, rhythmically.

'Brilliant!' said Cassie, then she copied him.

They practised again, adding in Alex's new moves. The frozen people in the audience looked like they were cheering them on. Cassie felt her heart flutter when she imagined all those people actually listening to them.

'. . . *Magic moments in our lives!*'

They sang the final line of the song for the last time and took a bow. Cassie waved to the frozen Jacey. It was time to make her wish come true!

'Bravo!' Comet barked. 'Now, any chance of a biscuit?'

Alex found a dog biscuit in his pocket and gave it to Comet as a thank you for his help.

'All this practice is hard work. It's

a good thing we had all the time in the world,' said Cassie, jingling her bracelet. 'But do you think we're ready to start time again, Alex?'

Alex nodded. 'Ready.'

Cassie looked at her butterfly charm and thought very hard. It sparkled, sending rainbows of colour into the air, and the tiny wings fluttered once more.

Immediately, everyone burst into life again. Noise and movement erupted all around Cassie. A group of older boys and girls

carried on dancing beside their friend, who was playing a guitar. People showed each other the bands listed in the festival programme, discussing who they wanted to watch. The woman's ice cream dripped on to the sand. Jacey wiped the tears from her eyes. Nothing had changed.

Except for one thing, Cassie thought.

'I hope Jacey thinks we're good enough,' she whispered to Alex.

'Of course she will,' Alex replied.

Cassie nodded. 'Jacey,' she said. 'I think Alex and I can help you. We could be your backing singers for "Magic Moments". Come on, we'll show you.'

★

When Cassie and Alex finished their demonstration to Jacey backstage, she clapped her hands and cheered.

'That was amazing! Cassie, your harmonies are wonderful. And your dance moves are brilliant, Alex,' Jacey said. 'What shall we do about costumes?'

Cassie exchanged a secret grin with Alex. 'We'll surprise you!' she said.

'You already *have* surprised me,' Jacey said, giving them both a big hug. 'Thank you so much. You've come to my rescue – and just in time!'

The festival manager was walking towards Jacey, pointing at his watch.

'Sorry, Miss Day, but you've run out of time. Shall I tell them it's cancelled?'

'No. No need to cancel,' Jacey said, a big smile lighting up her face. 'We've got a brand-new act. It might not be what the fans are expecting, but I know they're going to love it!'

Cassie felt so happy. Not only was she going to make Jacey's wish come true – she was going to sing and dance with her too. She couldn't wait to tell Kate and all her other friends. Some of them would be in the crowd watching!

It's going to be my very own magic moment! she thought.

7
Magic Moments

Cassie and Alex were backstage, wearing the costumes Cassie had stowed away. The festival organizers bustled around, putting the spotlights in position and testing the speaker system.

Jacey was standing by the stage entrance with a man wearing headphones. She gave Cassie and Alex a wave.

When everything was ready, the man turned to Jacey. 'Three, two, one – go!' he said.

Jacey strode on to the stage and the audience broke into wild cheers. Cassie and Alex peered around the entrance so they could see what was happening.

Jacey held up her hands and everyone quietened down.

'Thank you, Astral-on-Sea,' Jacey said into the microphone. 'I'm so happy to be opening the Songs on the Sand music festival!'

Another roar from the crowd filled the air.

'I'd like to sing you a very special song. In fact, it might have been written about the wonderful time I'm having here in this lovely town,' said Jacey. 'It's called "Magic Moments".'

The audience cheered, then went quiet again as Jacey continued.

'As you'll all know, I need my backing singers to sing the special harmony on "Magic Moments", but they couldn't make it here today.'

There was a disappointed sigh from the audience.

'However . . .' Jacey went on.

Cassie and Alex walked on to the stage, wearing their straw hats and big sunglasses. Jacey grinned at them.

'I'm so glad you're here,' she whispered. Then she turned to the crowd. 'Please welcome Cassie and Alex, my new backing singers. They're the Jacey Day Stars!'

The crowd cheered again and Cassie and Alex grinned at each other. Cassie spotted her mum and dad near the front. Their mouths were open in astonishment at seeing her on the stage with Jacey! Alex's parents were next to them, also looking surprised, and clapping excitedly. Cassie waved and blew

them all a kiss.

The band began to play and Jacey started to sing.

'There's a friend I'd love to meet . . .'

Cassie looked at Alex and gave him a nod. Then they both joined in, singing and dancing with Jacey and the band.

'*Spinning world beneath his feet . . .*'

Their voices sounded beautiful. The song seemed to flash by, until the last words hung in the air.

'*. . . Magic moments in our lives!*'

On the final note, an explosion of shooting stars, in violet and gold, orange and scarlet, poured over the stage like a twinkling snowstorm. The crowd went wild.

'Where did that glitter come from?' Jacey gasped.

Cassie smiled. She knew. *Stella Starkeeper*, she thought.

Jacey bowed and then beckoned to Cassie and Alex. Holding hands, they all bowed again. As they finished, the festival manager walked onstage and gave them each a beautiful bouquet of flowers. Cassie was so happy she thought she would burst.

Alex grinned at her. 'That was brilliant!' he whispered as they waved to the audience and left the stage.

'Better than singing in the bath?' Cassie teased.

While Jacey signed autographs, Cassie and Alex ran over to their parents.

'Congratulations,' said Alex's mum, shaking her head in amazement. 'You sounded really good.'

'They were fantastic,' Cassie's mum agreed.

'Never knew you could sing like that – must take after me,' said Alex's dad, winking at him.

'What I can't understand is when you got the time to practise,' said Jacey's mum, walking over from where she had been watching in the wings. She hugged Cassie and Alex, both at the same time. 'You two were magical.'

The two friends exchanged a secret smile. Cassie felt a tingling sensation on her wrist, and she looked down at her bracelet. With a burst of shimmering sparkles, a colourful flower appeared. She had earned her fourth charm. Now she was well on the way to

becoming a Lucky Star!

Cassie smiled to herself. *I wonder what magic this charm can do*, she thought.

Jacey finally finished signing autographs and came over to join Cassie and Alex. Flicking back her long hair, she kicked off her silver shoes and stood barefoot on the cool sand.

'Thank you for making my wish come true,' she said to Cassie. 'Is there anything I can do for you in return?'

Cassie looked thoughtful. 'Actually, there is something,' she said.

★

Cassie and Alex stood on the doorstep of the Fairy-cake Bakery. Comet, his tail wagging, sat next to them while Jacey stood quietly behind. Cassie knocked on the door.

Kate's mum opened it and gasped in surprise when she noticed Jacey. 'Aren't you the girl who sings "Magic Moments"?' she asked. 'My daughter loves that song.'

Jacey smiled. 'Yes I am, and thank you.'

'Is Kate well enough to have visitors?' Cassie asked.

'Of course, dear,' Kate's mum said.

They went upstairs and Cassie poked her head round the bedroom door. Kate was sitting up in bed, tucked under a quilt with a pretty cupcake pattern on it.

'Cassie!' Kate said, delighted to see her friend. 'Hi, Alex. Hi, Comet,' she added as they entered.

Cassie gave Kate a gentle hug. 'We've

got a surprise for you.'

She grinned as Jacey walked in and Kate's eyes opened wide in disbelief.

'Are you . . . ?' Kate gasped.

'Hello,' Jacey said, smiling at Kate. 'I heard you couldn't come to the festival, so Cassie thought we could bring the concert to you. You can hear my new Jacey Day Stars sing.'

Jacey, Cassie and Alex launched into the song. Kate clapped in time, joining in with Alex's rippling sound-wave dance move from her bed.

'And when I need a friendly face,
I know I'll come back to this place.
Starlight shimmering in the sky,
I will be there by and by.'

Seeing Kate's happy face made Cassie realize that there were many kinds of magic in the world, and they didn't all need charms to make them work.

They finished singing and Kate's mum walked in with a tray full of beautiful fairy cakes. As Cassie took a big bite of her cake, she noticed a shooting star flash past the window. Stella Starkeeper!

I can't wait for my next magical adventure, Cassie thought. *And to make someone else's wish come true.*

Cassie's Things to Make and Do!

Join in the Lucky Stars fun!

The Pop Singer Wish
True or False

I hope you enjoyed my Lucky Star story. How much do you remember?

My favourite singer Jacey Day's real name is Jacinta.

True ☆ or False? ☆

The song I sing on stage with Jacey is called 'Special Moments'.

True ☆ or False? ☆

Wishes really do come true
Lucky Stars

The new charm I get after making Jacey's wish come true is a flower.

True ☆ or False? ☆

My friend Kate lives at Daffodil Farm.

True ☆ or False? ☆

The name of the festival we performed at with Jacey Day was called Songs on the Sea.

True ☆ or False? ☆

Host a Talent Show

1. Gather together a group of your most talented friends.

2. Each friend has twenty minutes to come up with their talent. It could be: a song, a dance, a story, a drawing, a magic trick, a joke or even a gymnastics move . . . phew! It could be anything that's special to that person.

3. In preparation for the show you could make your own costumes, choose some music to walk in to, and even

create programmes to hand out to the audience. You could also make a stage area with a curtain or some lamps and plants.

4. Get everyone to sit in a row in front of the stage and let each person take their turn in the spotlight – each act should be about two to three minutes long. Be supportive and make sure you cheer each other on!

5. After each person has shown their talent, everyone must make a secret vote on a piece of paper for their favourite act – remember you can't vote for yourself!

6. When all the votes are in, one person must count them out and a winner will be decided. You can then hold an award ceremony for the best talent (copy the trophy design shown opposite on to a piece of card and cut it out to use as the prize). There doesn't just have to be one winner. You could also give an award to the funniest talent or the most creative! Then the winners might want to make a speech where they thank lots of people and talk about their inspirations!

Answers

Don't look unless you're really stuck!

The Pop Singer Wish True or False

True, False, True, False, False.

Wishes really do come true

Lucky Stars

The Birthday Wish

To read an exciting chapter,

please turn the page . . .

1
The Great Fandango

'Snap!' said Cassie, putting a matching card on the pile. 'I'm going to win this time.'

'We'll see about that,' said Alex. He grinned and put down another card.

It was a rainy day in Astral-on-Sea. Cassie and Alex were playing a game of Snap in her bedroom at Starwatcher Towers. Cassie's parents owned the Starwatcher Towers Bed and Breakfast, and Alex was there on holiday with his family, including his little white puppy, Comet. Alex and Cassie had become firm friends.

'SNAP!' Alex shouted. 'That's two games to me and one to you. You see, it's all about probability.'

'Probability?' Cassie repeated.

'It's a theory scientists use to work out how often something might happen,' Alex replied. 'I'm working out how often the cards come up in pairs by counting the cards in between.'

Cassie smiled. Only Alex would know a scientific way to play Snap.

'I think you're just lucky!' she said.

She looked up at the glass roof of her bedroom and sighed. It curved round into a dome shape just like the roof of her dad's observatory. At night, Cassie liked watching the stars through the glass roof, but now all she could see were raindrops falling with a steady pitter-pat.

'It's raining too hard to go out,' she said,

stroking Twinkle, her old black cat. He purred happily. 'What if someone's making a wish? How will I know if I'm stuck indoors?' she wondered aloud.

'You've already helped make three people's wishes come true,' Alex pointed out. 'So the probability is that you'll somehow manage to help a fourth person.'

Twinkle nuzzled Cassie's arm and the charms on her bracelet tinkled together. Stella Starkeeper, Cassie's magical friend, had given her the silver bracelet for her seventh birthday a few days before. Every time Cassie helped to make someone's wish come true, she received another charm with a new magical power. So far, she had four charms – with the bird charm she could fly, with the crescent moon she could speak to animals, and with the butterfly she could freeze time. Her newest charm was a flower, but she didn't know yet what its magic power was. When she earned seven charms she would become a real Lucky Star, like Stella. Then she would be able to grant any wish she liked! But Cassie knew she had a lot to do before that magical day.

Cassie looked at the grey sky. There was no sign of Stella Starkeeper among the clouds.

She heard Alex's tummy growl noisily.

'I'm hungry,' he said.

'I'm hungry too,' Cassie agreed. 'Let's go and get some breakfast.'

Cassie carried Twinkle downstairs to the dining room where she and Alex tucked into boiled eggs and toast.

'I wonder if it will ever stop raining today,' Cassie said with a sigh.

'Ahem,' a new voice chipped in. 'May I join you? I think I could make your grey day disappear!'

Cassie turned round in surprise to see who had spoken. There stood a boy, a little taller than Alex, wearing a top hat and a black cape. He gave them a cheeky grin. Cassie recognized him as one of the new bed-and-breakfast guests.

'Yes, of course you can join us,' Cassie said. 'I'm Cassie and this is Alex.'

The new boy bowed and his shiny black cape swung around his shoulders, revealing a bright red lining.

'I am the Great Fandango,' he announced.

'That's a very unusual name,' Alex said.

'My real name's Marcus Chen,' Marcus told them. 'The Great Fandango is my stage name. I chose "Fandango" because it sounds magical, and "Great" because that's what I want my tricks to be.'

'You're a magician!' Cassie said excitedly.

'Yes,' said Marcus.

'I'm going to be a scientist,' said Alex.

'Wow,' Marcus said, 'that's *great* too.'

Cassie and Alex laughed.

'Why have you got your magician's outfit on?' Alex asked.

'I'm doing a magic show at my cousin Lia's birthday party,' Marcus explained. 'She's five today. I don't see her very often because we live far away. The magic show is my birthday present to her.'

'What a brilliant idea,' Alex said.

'Do you like magic?' asked Marcus.

Cassie and Alex grinned at one another. They certainly liked the magical adventures they had using the charms on Cassie's bracelet.

'We love magic,' Cassie said.

With a flourish, Marcus pulled out a

black wand with a white tip. 'Then I shall show you my magic tricks,' he said.

He turned the bottom of Alex's empty eggshell upside down on the plate. Then he shook out a clean napkin and carefully covered the empty shell.

As she watched Marcus prepare his trick, Cassie noticed a glimmer of sunshine through the dining-room window. It made the streaks of rainwater on the windows gleam like diamonds.

This could turn out to be quite a magical day after all, she thought with a smile.

Wishes really do come true
Lucky Stars

Explore the magical world of Lucky Stars!

For fun things to make and do – as well as games and quizzes – go to:

www.luckystarsbooks.co.uk